Doing Christmas

PUFFIN BOOKS

Published by the Penguin Group
Penguin Books Ltd, 27 Wrights Lane, London W8 5TZ, England
Penguin Books USA Inc., 375 Hudson Street, New York, New York 10014, USA
Penguin Books Australia Ltd, Ringwood, Victoria, Australia
Penguin Books Canada Ltd, 10 Alcorn Avenue, Toronto, Ontario, Canada M4V 3B2
Penguin Books (NZ) Ltd, 182–190 Wairau Road, Auckland 10, New Zealand

Penguin Books Ltd, Registered Offices: Harmondsworth, Middlesex, England

First published by The Bodley Head 1994
Published in Puffin Books 1996
1 3 5 7 9 10 8 6 4 2

SARAH GARLAND

Doing Christmas

PUFFIN BOOKS

Granny is coming for Christmas.

We will do the shopping,

and boil the pudding,

and dig up the tree,

and get everything ready for Christmas.

It is Christmas Day and here comes Granny.

She is early.

She has brought some presents.

Granny tells stories

until lunchtime.

Then we walk to the park.

It is time to say goodbye.

It is the end of Christmas Day.